Best Wishes!

When Dog Pals Fly across America

ROB KORTUS

A Gift for:

_____

From:

_____

Date:

_____

To Mom and Dad

Thank you for your unconditional love

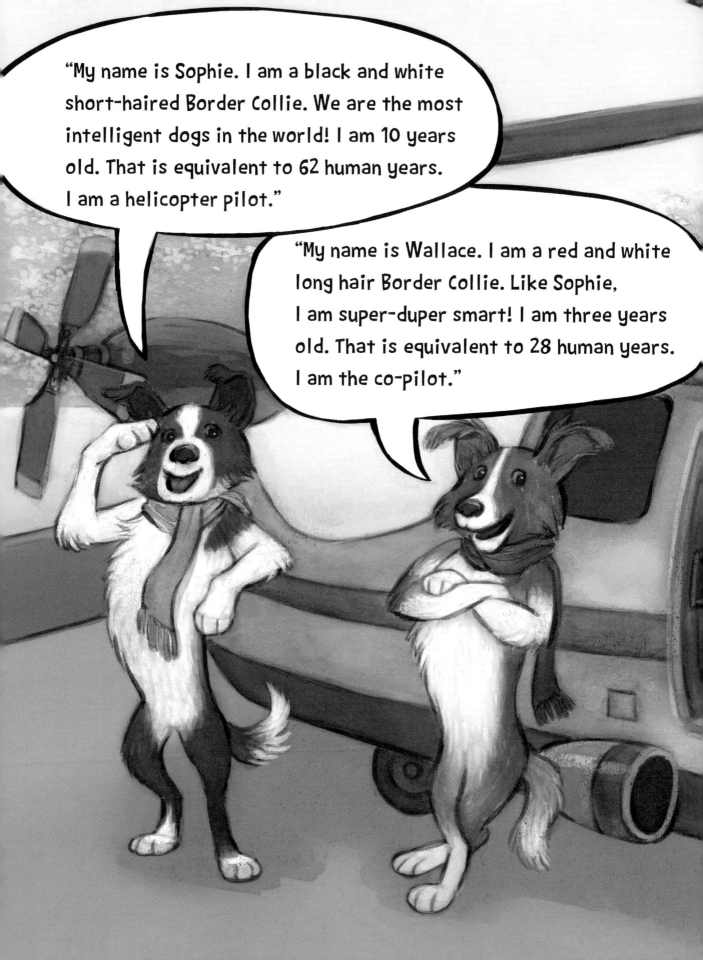

"Okay flight crew, we are going to fly to each state in the United States of America and see some cool places! Ready for take-off.
All systems green."

"Check out that underwater hotel in Key Largo, FL!
This is where the Jules Undersea Lodge hotel is!
You have to scuba dive to get to the lodge!"

"Tank Town in Morganton, GA where you can drive a tank and crash cars!"

"Look! It is Stumphouse Tunnel near Wallhalla, SC! This tunnel was supposed to be a shortcut for a railway but government cut funding so Clemson used it to make blue cheese! Now, just a public place to venture into but watch out for the bats!"

"Look at the beautiful feral Colonial Spanish Mustangs in Corolla, NC!"

"Wow! Check out the 20 foot high 43 giant busts of the presidents in the field below in Croaker, VA!"

Pennsylvania

Ohio

West Virginia

Virginia

"It's the National Radio Observatory in Green Bank, WV! It's the world's largest steerable telescope! Let's go inside!"

"Look! The Petersen House in DC where President Lincoln died. There is a 34 foot tall stack of books three floors high dedicated to the 16th president. 6,800 books!"

Pennsylvania
Maryland
Delaware
Washington D.C.
Virginia

"Wow! Graffiti Alley in Baltimore, MD!
Look at all of the colors!"

"It's Jersey Shore Pirates in Brick Township, NJ! Let's be pirates!"

"Neat! Ice castles in North Woodstock, NH! I bet you it is cold inside!"

"It's Track 61 which is now abandoned below the Waldorf-Astoria hotel in New York, NY. It was allegedly used to secretly transport presidents. Lots of important people used Track 61!"

"Look at the Philadelphia's Moon Tree in PA! The tree is a clone-tree growing in Washington Square Park and was sprung from seeds that went to the moon and back with the astronauts in the 1970's."

New York

Pennsylvania

Ohio

Maryland

West Virginia

"That looks like fun! Airboat rides in Sandusky, OH! Way cool!"

"It's the Holland Festival in Holland, MI!
So many beautiful flowers!"

Michigan

Indiana   Ohio

"Look at the Exotic Feline Rescue Center in Center Point, IN! They are playful gentle giants."

"It's Mooseheart Child City and School in Mooseheart, IL! The author's father grew up here when it was an orphanage. Richard used to live in the New Jersey residence. Let's go play with the kids!"

Iowa

Illinois   Indiana

Missouri

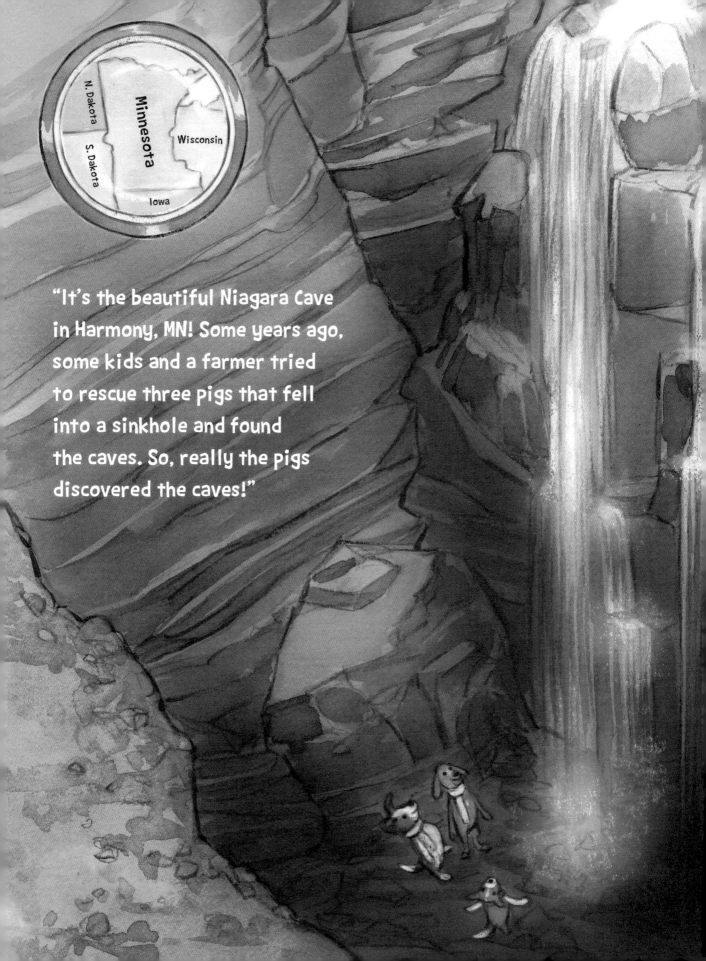

"It's the beautiful Niagara Cave in Harmony, MN! Some years ago, some kids and a farmer tried to rescue three pigs that fell into a sinkhole and found the caves. So, really the pigs discovered the caves!"

N. Dakota

S. Dakota

Minnesota

Wisconsin

Iowa

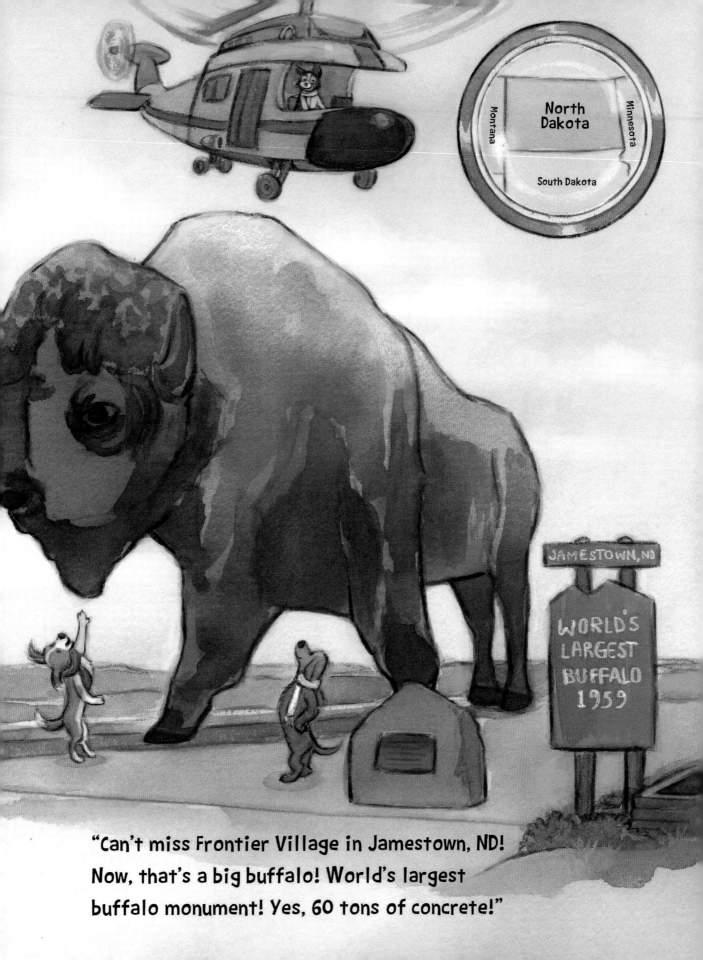

"Can't miss Frontier Village in Jamestown, ND! Now, that's a big buffalo! World's largest buffalo monument! Yes, 60 tons of concrete!"

"Wow! The Dinosaur Trail stretches from Bynum to Ekalaka MT! Time to stretch our legs and take a hike."

"It's America's largest sea cave! Look! Sea Lions Cave in Florence, OR! Those sea lions are so playful!"

Washington

Oregon

Idaho

California   Nevada

"Bubblegum Alley in San Luis Obispo, CA! People have stuck their bubblegum on these walls for years! Isn't that funny and cool!"

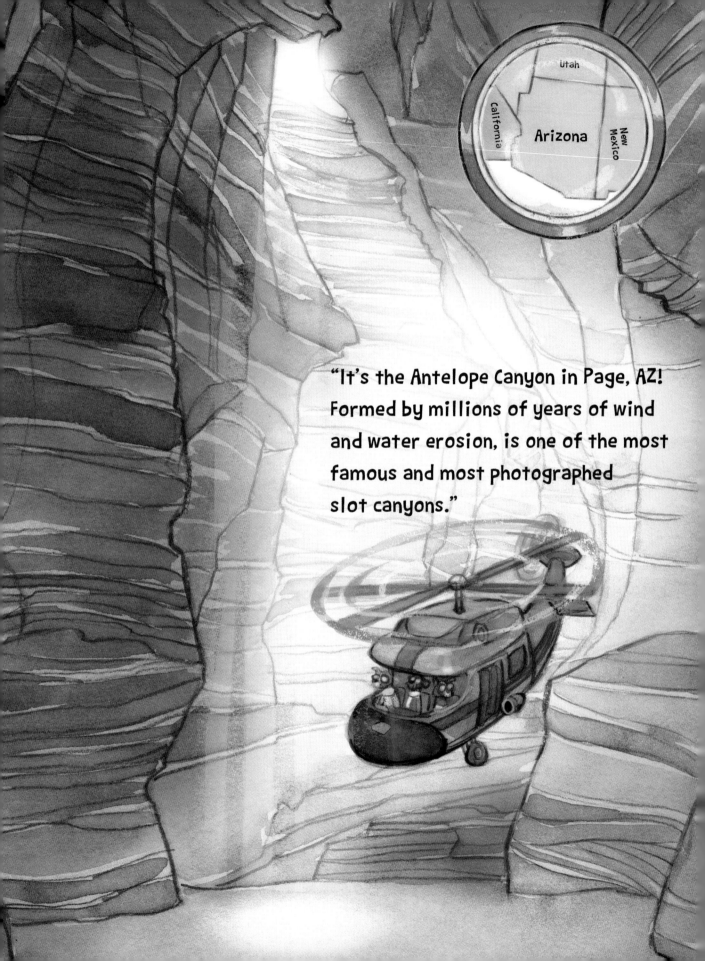

"It's the Antelope Canyon in Page, AZ! Formed by millions of years of wind and water erosion, is one of the most famous and most photographed slot canyons."

Utah

California

Arizona

New Mexico

"Watch out! Don't fly into the balloons! So many colors! It's the International Balloon Fiesta in Albuquerque, NM!"

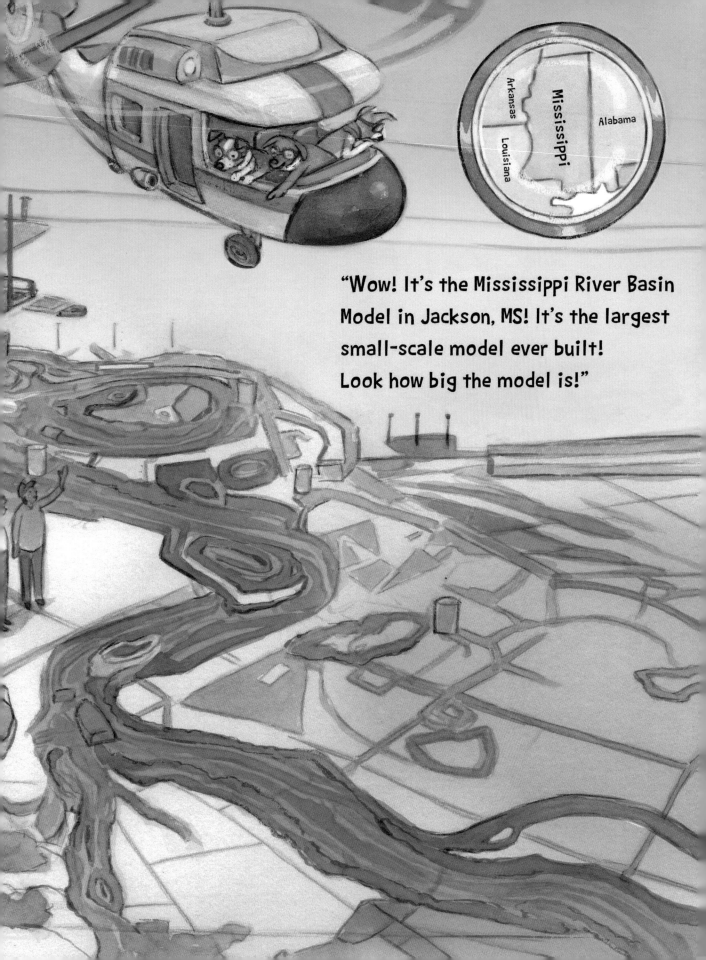

"Wow! It's the Mississippi River Basin Model in Jackson, MS! It's the largest small-scale model ever built! Look how big the model is!"

"Wow! It's K'REX in Huntsville, AL. It's 12 feet tall, 33 feet long, and nearly six feet wide! According to the Guinness World Records, 141,950 K'Nex pieces were used!"

"Cool! Gentry Farm in Franklin, TN! Look at the maze! Look at all of the kids and dogs trying to find their way out!"

"Hey! It's the spinach capitol of the world!
There's the bronze statue of Popeye in Alma, AR!"

"Let's stop in the Matchstick Marvel Museum in Gladbrook, IA! That is amazing!"

"Skeleton Man Walking Skeleton Dinosaur in SD! Cool! Is that a T-Rex? Oh my gosh! It's a man walking his prehistoric dinosaur."

"Cool! The Greyhound Hall of Fame in Abiline, KS! Those dogs are fast!"

"Let's play on the Playtower in Bartlesville, OK. This tower was inspired by the space age."

Kansas

Oklahoma

Arkansas

Texas

"It's Swetsville Zoo in Fort Collins, CO!
Those are some funny looking animals!"

"The Tree Rock in Buford, WY! The tree is actually growing out of a boulder! Smallest town in Wyoming. Population 1. I would be lonely."

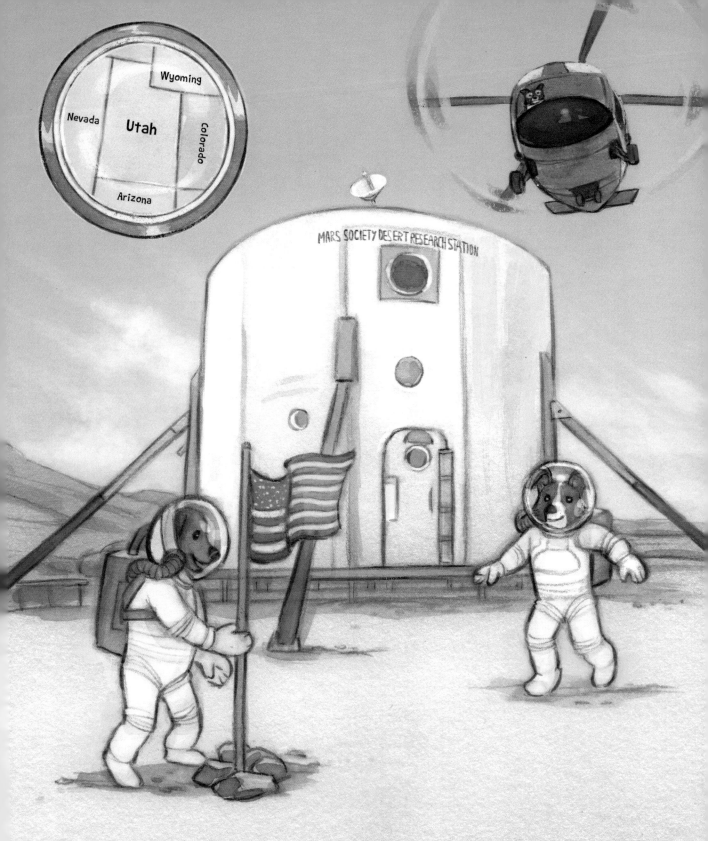

"Cool! It's the Mars Desert Research Station in Hanksville, UT! Astronauts practice things like they are on Mars."

"Wow! The Shoe Tree in Fallon, NV!
Look at all of the shoes in the tree!"

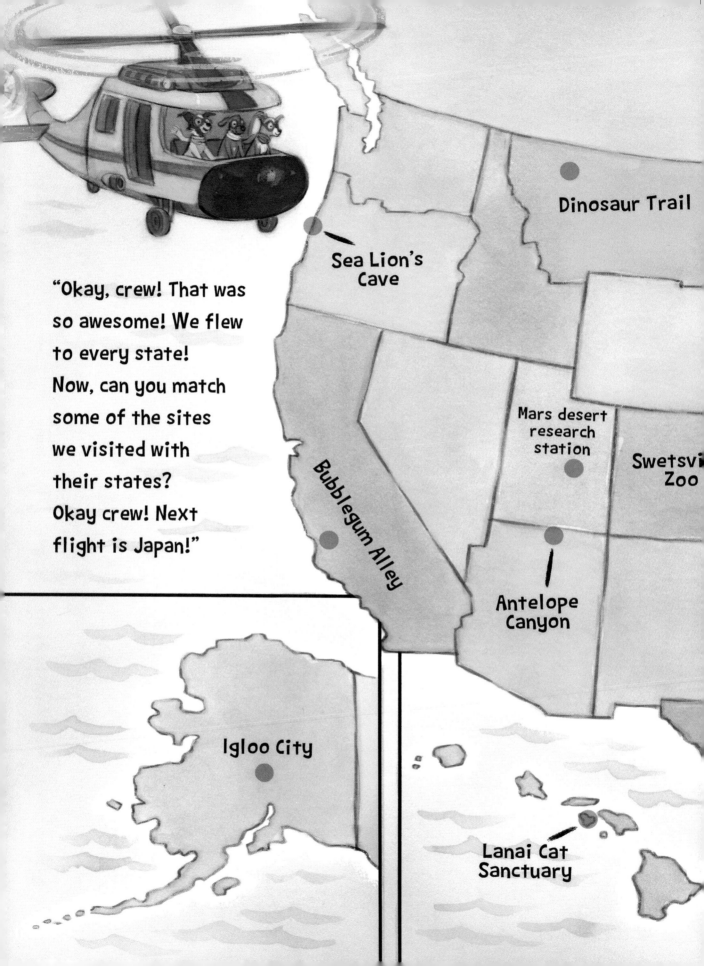

Rob Kortus is a retired Coast Guard helicopter pilot and Advanced Master Dog Educator and Trainer. He holds a Bachelor of Science in Professional Aeronautics and a Master of Arts in Organizational Management.
As a highly experienced helicopter pilot and dog trainer, Rob has created this delightful children's book with his personal canine companions as the characters. Sophie the Border Collie, Sulley the Chocolate Lab mix, and Wallace the Border Collie. In this first series of When Dog Pals Fly, his three dogs take flight in their personal helicopter and make stopovers in every state in the USA to visit a cool place that readers of all ages will enjoy! This is a first book in a series of books where Sophie, Sulley, and Wallace will fly to every country in the world!

Rob lives and works out of his home in Charlotte, NC with his three loving canines. If you would like a book signing, contact Rob and the pups via the website (www.whendogpalsfly.com) where you can personally meet Rob, Sophie, Sulley, and Wallace! The book characters can't wait to meet you and take their photos with you!

Your positive Amazon book review would be greatly appreciated. Thank you for your purchase. Rob & Pups